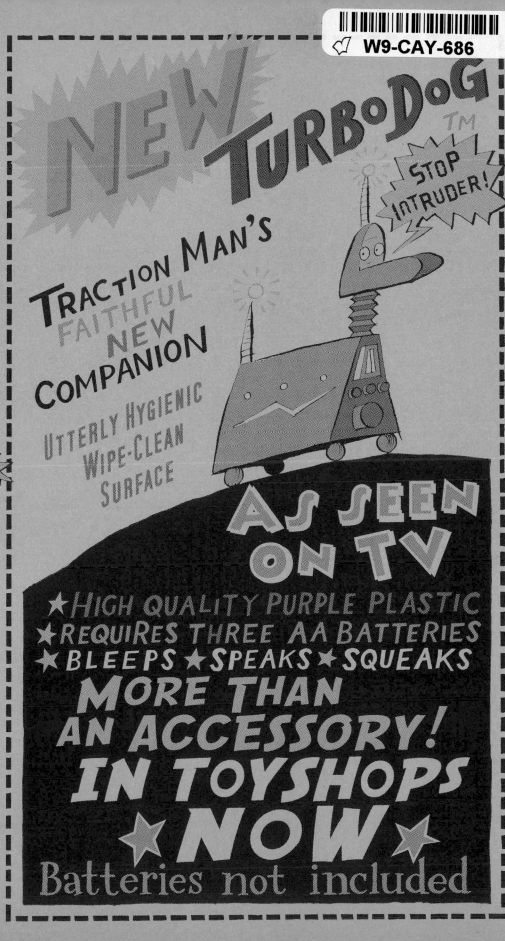

Traction Man
meets
Turbodog
Mini Grey

ALFRED A. KNOPF
New York

...and PLEASE stay out of the mud today.

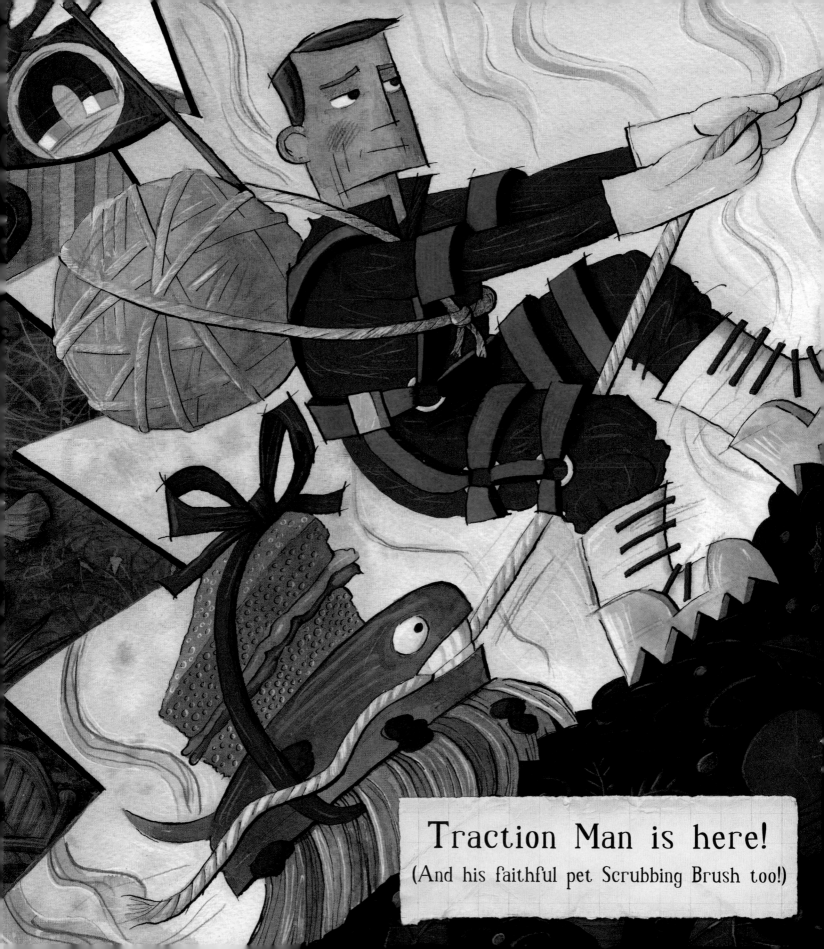

Traction Man is here!
(And his faithful pet Scrubbing Brush too!)

They have to pass through the ring of Mystic Shrooms.

BOW LOW YOU MUST

They bow to the Shrooms.

The Summit!

They plant a flag and have their sandwich.

The only way back is through the swampy marshes of the Pond.

They can cross by Boot.

Traction Man and Scrubbing Brush are drying off in front of the heater.

Traction Man is wearing a knotted spotted hanky.

Scrubbing Brush is encrusted with dried-on dirt.

Everyone is warm and sleepy.

Traction Man and Turbodog are crossing the wastes of the Sandpit.

Somewhere under the shifting sands are the ruins of the Handbag.

Maybe that's a corner of it there.
The Handbag Dwellers are very shy.

Traction Man and Turbodog are watching Turbodog's greatest adventures on TV.

Turbodog thinks it is just getting to the good bit.
This is what Turbodog likes to do BEST.

STOP INTRUDER!

Scrubbing Brush!
I must find my brave pet!
Where can Scrubbing Brush be?

Traction Man is searching in their favorite hiding places.

The toy cupboard . . .

Under the bed . . .

He wears his Airtight Astro-Suit
with Glass Head-Globe.
The atmosphere at the Bin's surface
may be deadly poisonous.

Traction Man takes
a bottle of
**SuperStrong
GERMO**
(with Ammonia).

No one has ever
returned alive from
the Bin before.

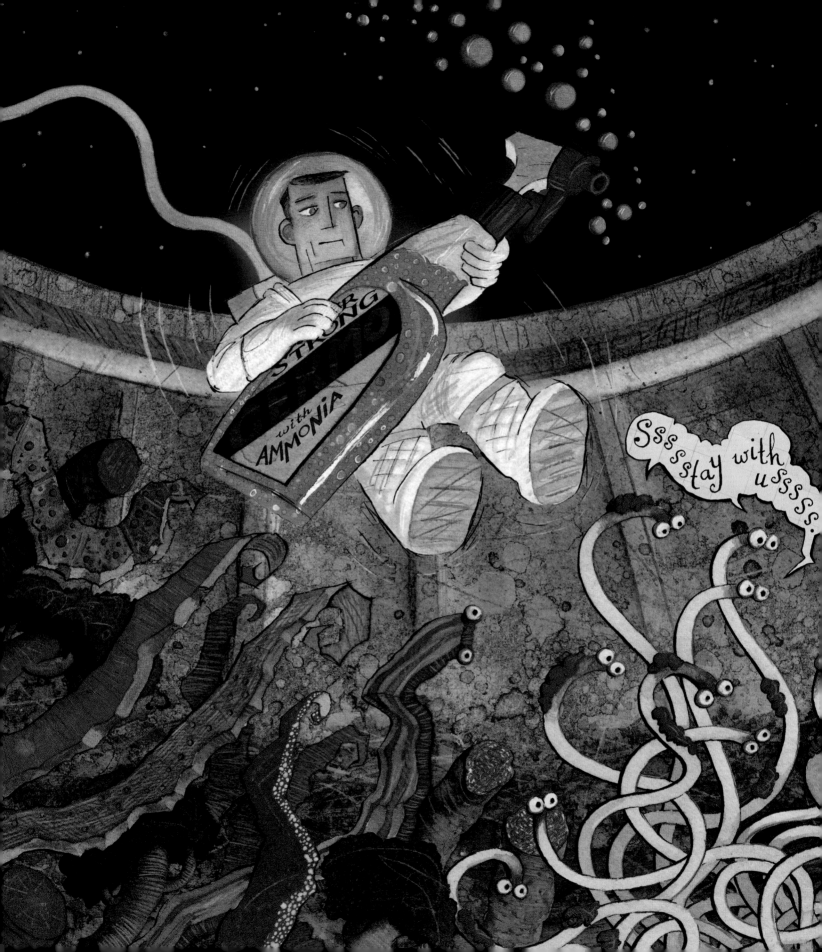

There's a fizz and a flicker.

CLUNK

Oh dear.

Traction Man and Scrubbing Brush are
Surviving for the afternoon in the
shrubbery near the Pond.
Traction Man has his Magnetic Compass,
First-Aid Kit and Survival Vest.
They have constructed a shelter from
pillowcases and a bath mat.

The Dollies are looking after Turbodog.
He is very quiet now. (They had to
take out his rusty batteries.)

Scrubbing Brush is wearing a
Badge of Cleanness
and has been foraging for Supplies.
Traction Man is helping
Scrubbing Brush to stay clean.
And of course, they are both
Prepared for
Anything.

A Present for SCRUBBING BRUSH from Dad

This book is dedicated to Ian Craig.

THIS IS A BORZOI BOOK PUBLISHED BY ALFRED A. KNOPF

Copyright © 2008 by Mini Grey

Visit us on the Web! www.randomhouse.com/kids

Educators and librarians, for a variety of teaching tools, visit us at www.randomhouse.com/teachers

Library of Congress Cataloging-in-Publication Data
Grey, Mini.
Traction Man meets Turbodog / by Mini Grey. — 1st American ed.
p. cm.
Summary: Traction Man, an action figure, teams up with the high-tech but not-so-bright Turbodog to rescue
Scrubbing Brush, his missing sidekick, from the terrible underworld of the bin.
ISBN 978-0-375-85583-2 (trade) — ISBN 978-0-375-95583-9 (lib. bdg.)
[1. Action figures (Toys)—Fiction. 2. Brooms and brushes—Fiction. 3. Toys—Fiction.
4. Lost and found possessions—Fiction.] I. Title.
PZ7.G873Trm 2008
[E]—dc22
2007041525

MANUFACTURED IN MALAYSIA
September 2008
10 9 8 7 6 5 4 3 2 1

First American Edition

THE MYSTERIOUS SHROOMS
WOULD LIKE TO THANK
STEVE COLE FOR HIS HELP
WITH THEIR LOAMWORK.

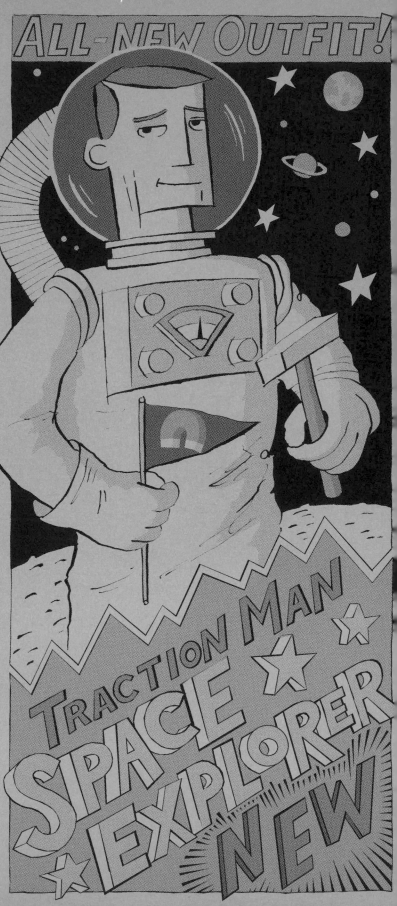